Adventures That Lead To Home

Written by Bonita Jewel Hele

Illustrated by Lisa Butler

Hartlyn Kids

There it was! He could see the light of his village in the distance. Rohit was overjoyed. He was home! The sun had almost set and he quickened his pace, eager to get home and greet his family, which included his parents and three younger siblings: Priya, his sister, was eight years old; Praveen, his brother, was six, and Mana was still a baby boy. How he had missed them. The memories of the past two days flew through his head. The teeth, the claws, the train, the cars, the food, the sights, the bewilderment—all these things were branded on his nine-year-old mind. Oh, he couldn't wait to get home and tell his family of his adventures!

Rohit's smile broadened as he neared his small village, which was nestled in the foothills near the mountains of northern India. He always enjoyed sitting beside the calm river watching the cows, water buffaloes, goats, sheep, and donkeys roam. After Rohit and his friends finished their chores, they would play games in the rice paddies or at times get lost in the great forest, which stretched past the agricultural fields.

He ran past the huts and through the village clearing, jumping over stray chickens clucking around. On his way home he ran into Samir, one of his school friends, who was returning from working in the fields with his father before supper.

"Rohit, Rohit," yelled Samir, running towards him. "We really missed you! Did you enjoy your first trip to the big city?"

"Yes," Rohit replied, "In fact, I am rushing home at this moment to fill my family in on my adventure! Did anything exciting happen while I was in Nagpur visiting my cousin, aunt and uncle?"

Samir responded with excitement, "Oh, yes! We had quite a scare yesterday. My little brother attempted to collect river water for our baths and got the surprise of his life!"

"Ah yes," said Rohit. "He came across his first crocodile! I am sure he will wait patiently for your father to bring his bath water from now on." Rohit and Samir both laughed and Rohit continued at a swift pace to go home to see his family.

He ran and ran until he was standing outside the door of his hut. He called out in Hindi with a loud voice, "*Ma, Pithaji, main hoon na!*" In English this means, "Mom, Dad, I'm here!"

His father and mother came out to meet him wearing big smiles on their faces. Rohit respectfully touched his father's feet in greeting before jumping into his mother's arms. His father patted his back as his mother held him close. "*Main aapse pyaar kartha hoon!*" she said. This means, "I love you!"

Rohit stepped back and looked at both his parents. "Oh boy, I have so much to tell you!"

After the night meal, the family gathered around the light of a kerosene lamp, snuggling on their sleeping mats on the cool dirt floor of the hut. Rohit's father broke the silence. "So, tell us about your trip, son. Did you enjoy yourself?"

Rohit was quick to answer. "Oh yes, Pithaji! I have so much to tell you! After Ma woke me up, I was a little nervous about my trip. I was so excited that I rushed through my breakfast, got my things together, and ran out the door..."

"And you left so fast you nearly forgot to say goodbye to me," his father gently chided with a smile on his face.

Rohit blushed and then continued. "But it's a good thing you called me back, because the advice you gave me saved my life! But I'm not at that part of the story yet."

His mother and father looked at each other in alarm. Saved his life? What did he mean?

Rohit continued his story. "It was a beautiful, sunny day! There were lots of birds and monkeys chattering in the trees. I saw a few deer and a mongoose, too. But I hardly paid any attention to them as I was in a hurry to reach the train. I decided to follow the worn prints of the animals, knowing it would lead to the lake at the other side of the forest. After walking for an hour in the forest, I came within sight of the clearing that led to the lake! I was so happy that I started to run toward it. However, it was then that I heard it."

"Heard what?" Praveen, his brother, interrupted.

"There was the sound of rustling leaves behind me and I heard a few twigs break. I smelled the air and I knew instantly what it was. It was only a few weeks ago that Pithaji had taken me to the place where one of them had killed our milk buffalo. He taught me its scent..."

His father looked at him in surprise. "You came across a tiger? What did you do? Were you scared?"

"Oh, I was terrified! My heart was pounding so loudly, I thought surely the tiger could hear it. I felt faint and wanted to run away! But I remembered Pithaji's words about how to ward off a tiger. And so I fought my fear and turned slowly and faced it, looking it squarely in the eye. I looked at it for what seemed to be forever. I fully expected the tiger to rush toward me and gobble me up!

But I kept staring, and at last the tiger turned and walked away into the forest."

Rohit was shaking at the memory of his encounter. His mother hugged him as his father patted his shoulder. "You're a brave one, my son!" he said.

Rohit smiled at the memory. "I ran as fast as I could until I reached the train tracks. I finally got to the tracks at a few minutes after ten. I worried the train had passed and I would lose my chance to visit my cousin and the city. So I was excited when I saw the train in the distance approaching. I waited until it was passing me and I then ran alongside it until I reached an open door. I grabbed onto it and swung myself inside. I quietly found a seat and sat down. I was hoping to enjoy the view, but I was so worn out from my trip that I fell fast asleep."

"I can imagine that you were," his mother said. "I hope that things were a little bit calmer after that."

"Oh no, Ma! The adventure had only begun! I arrived at the train station and jumped out onto the platform, looking for Prakash and his family. I couldn't see them, so I ran toward the exit looking for them, dodging luggage, baggage boys and stray dogs in my way. However, I couldn't find them at all! I looked from one end of the platform to the other and then back outside again. All I could see were people—thousands of them—but no familiar faces. I started to feel afraid. I wondered if they forgot that I was coming. So I sat and thought for a while, and I decided that I would try to find them. After my encounter with the tiger, I felt ready for any adventure." He smiled. His mother shook her head, while his father laughed.

Rohit continued, "I left the station and walked out of the parking lot through a large crowd of auto-rickshaw drivers who were arguing very loudly. They were trying to attra the best passengers to give a ride to their destination. Once I got outside that racket, I was amazed at what I saw, all the sights and sounds. Here in the village we see trees around us; there all I could see were big buildings rising high. Our companions here are animals or people on carts; the city roads were filled with cars of all different sizes and colors. Everything seemed so different! Only the occasional cow or stray dog running down the road kept me from believing that I had landed on a different planet." He laughed at his own joke. His siblings were listening with wide-eyed wonder.

began to walk down the road, trying to figure out what to do. However, I was soon
⋯t and decided to ask around for help. The first person who stopped was a really
⋯e man! I asked him for help and told him my story. You know what's weird? Here
⋯ know where everyone lives but in the city, no one knows where other people live!
⋯e man had no idea where aunt and uncle lived!"

⋯ father spoke up. "Son, we have five hundred people in our village. Nagpur has
⋯er two million people living there. That's a slight difference." He winked at Rohit.

"Anyway, the man then asked if I knew their phone number and if he should call them. I didn't understand what he meant by that. He must have seen that I was confused because he pulled this little contraption called a cell phone out of his pocket. He laughed when he saw me staring. He handed me his cell phone to look at. He said that with this thing, you could reach anyone, anywhere, at any time if you had their phone number. We need to get some of those things here!"

Within a few minutes, he had found uncle's number and called him to come and get me. They showed up a few minutes later. Prakash ran up to me and said how sorry he was that they did not make it to the station. Somehow they got the times mixed up and they were not expecting me to arrive until later in the evening. We all thanked the kind man who had helped me. I followed Prakash and his father to a fancy, huge car! I have never traveled so fast in my life, but I enjoyed the trip!"

His father said, "That car sounds like it sure beats an ox cart any day!" Rohit nodded.

Then Rohit said, "It was late afternoon when we got home. You have to see their house! It was tall with many rooms; the walls were smooth and covered with paint. Our village homes are simple, made of stone with a thatched roof. I didn't know buildings such as these were possible. They took me to the room upstairs that I would be sharing with Prakash for the weekend. It had lots of nice furniture and toys and games. There was also a computer, which Prakash showed me how to use. After I took a nice warm bath, I watched Prakash play on the computer for some time."

His father asked, "Did you enjoy playing with Prakash and his toys?"

Rohit responded thoughtfully, "It was fun for a while, but then I started to get a bit bored. I thought about our home in the village. This was the time of day that I would play with my friends. We had just started a cricket tournament in the village and last week I hit my first 'six'! But Prakash has no brothers or sisters, and he seemed to be happy with his toys. Although I was enjoying myself, I began to miss home."

Rohit continued, "Dinner was soon ready and we both ran down and sat at the table. Before us was a feast. I don't think I have ever eaten so much! Oh, and guess what we had after dinner? Ice cream! And auntie let me have two servings! After eating, we headed back upstairs, thoroughly stuffed. Prakash pulled out a board game and we soon were playing together. We finished our game and then got ready for bed. Prakash's mom came to tuck us in for the night. Oh, we slept on beds too — not sleeping mats!"

"That sounds like a lot of fun, Rohit!" It was Priya, his sister. "Do you wish that you also lived in the city, like Prakash?"

Rohit thought about it for a moment. The chirping of crickets was the only sound as everyone waited to hear what Rohit had to say. He finally spoke. "No, I would not like to go live in the city like Prakash. Although I had a wonderful time there, I also came to realize that koie jaga ghar jaisey nahai hain. There is no place like home!"

His mother and father smiled as they hugged him tight. Seeing that the hour was late, his father blew out the lamp and they settled down for the night. As his mother kissed him to sleep, he thought once more about the past few days. Tomorrow would be another day, and he knew now more than ever that "*koie jaga ghar jaisey nahai hain*"— there is no place like home!

LEARNING TOOLS

MA: mother.

PITHAJI: dad.

MAIN HOON NA: I'm here!

MAIN AAPSE PYAAR KARTHA HOON: I love you!

CRICKET: a bat-and-ball team sport. A six is scored when the
ball goes over the boundary rope without touching
the ground.

OJE JAGA GHAR JAISEY NAHAI HAIN: There is no place like home!

NAGPUR: a city in the state of Maharashtra, the largest city in
cantral India, and the third largest city by population in the
state of Maharashtra.

GONDWANA EXPRESS: a super fast train in India.